KU-321-501

阿里巴巴與四十大盜

Ali Baba *and the* Forty Thieves

Retold by Enebor Attard

Illustrated by Richard Holland

Chinese translation by Sylvia Denham

MORAY COUNCIL LIBRARIES & INFO.SERVICES	
2O 19 89 16	
Askews	
JB	

Mantra Lingua

在很久以前的阿拉伯，一個月圓的晚上，當阿里巴巴收拾點火的柴枝時，
他察覺到一些非常奇怪的事，他聽到一股好像雷聲的隆隆巨響，
它並非來自天上，而是從地底深處發出的。

A long time ago in Arabia, on a full moon night, Ali Baba noticed something very
strange as he gathered firewood. A rumbling sound, like thunder, came not from
the sky, but from below the earth.

更令阿里巴巴驚奇的是一塊巨石自動地滾動，
顯露出一個黑暗的山洞。

And to Ali Baba's astonishment, a gigantic rock
rolled across on its very own, revealing a dark cave.

月光橫掃岩石所造成的奇形怪狀的影子，阿里巴巴感覺到那裏不只他一個人，他爬近一些，差點兒跌倒在一群等候著騎士的馬匹之前。
阿里巴巴躲藏起來，不久便有一群披了抖蓬的影子從洞中向著他直衝出來。

The moonlight sent strange shadows across the rocks. Ali Baba felt he was not alone.
He crept closer and nearly fell upon a pack of horses waiting for their riders.
Ali Baba hid and it was not long before a bunch of shadowy cloaks and hoods came out of the cave towards him.

他們是等待著首領卡伊的大盜。
當卡伊出現時，他望著星星叫道：「芝麻關門！」那塊巨石顫動著，
跟著便慢慢地滾回原處，將洞口隱蔽，把它的秘密收藏起來，
不讓全世界知道⋯除了阿里巴巴一個。

They were thieves waiting outside for Ka-eed, their leader.
When Ka-eed appeared, he looked towards the stars and howled out, "Close Sesame!"
The huge rock shook and then slowly rolled back, closing the mouth of the cave,
hiding its secret from the whole world... apart from Ali Baba.

當眾人消失後，阿里巴巴用力去推那塊石頭，它穩固地擱在那裏，
好像世界上沒有任何東西可以移動它似的。
「芝麻開門！」阿里巴巴細聲說。
那巨石慢慢地滾開，顯露出那個黑暗陰深的山洞。阿里巴巴盡量靜悄悄地走動，
但是每一步都發出響亮空洞的聲音，並到處產生回音，跟著他跌倒了，
跌跌撞撞的倒落在一堆刺繡華麗的絲織地氈上，他的周圍都是一袋袋的金幣
和銀幣，一瓶瓶的鑽石和綠寶石，更有大花瓶，裏面裝滿著… 更多的金幣。

When the men were out of sight, Ali Baba gave the rock a mighty push.
It was firmly stuck, as if nothing in the world could ever move it.
"Open Sesame!" Ali Baba whispered.
Slowly the rock rolled away, revealing the dark deep cave. Ali Baba tried to move
quietly but each footstep made a loud hollow sound that echoed everywhere.
Then he tripped. Tumbling over and over and over he landed on a pile of richly
embroidered silk carpets. Around him were sacks of gold and silver coins, jars of
diamond and emerald jewels, and huge vases filled with... even more gold coins!

「這是不是在造夢呢？」阿里巴巴驚奇地說。他拿起一條鑽石項鏈，
閃耀的鑽石刺痛他的眼睛，他將項鏈帶在頸上，跟著扣上另一條，又另一條，
他將他的襪子塞滿了珠寶，並在每個袋口都擠滿金塊，令他差不多不能將自己拖行出洞，
一旦出了洞口，他便轉身叫道：「芝麻關門！」那塊石頭便緊密地關上了。
你可以想像到阿里巴巴花了很多時間才返到家中。當他的妻子見到他的重負時，
她喜極而泣，現在他們有足夠一生享用的金錢財富了！

"Is this a dream?" wondered Ali Baba. He picked up a diamond necklace and the
sparkle hurt his eyes. He put it around his neck. Then he clipped on another, and
another. He filled his socks with jewels. He stuffed every pocket with so much
gold that he could barely drag himself out of the cave.
Once outside, he turned and called, "Close Sesame!" and the rock shut tight.
As you can imagine Ali Baba took a long time to get home. When his wife saw
the load she wept with joy. Now, there was enough money for a whole lifetime!

第二天，阿里巴巴將所發生的一切告訴他的兄弟卡深。
「切勿再走近那個山洞，」卡深警告他說，「那裏實在太危險了。」
卡深是否擔心他的兄弟的安全呢？不是，絕對不是。

The next day, Ali Baba told his brother, Cassim, what had happened.
"Stay away from that cave," Cassim warned. "It is too dangerous."
Was Cassim worried about his brother's safety? No, not at all.

那天晚上，當每個人都睡著了時，卡深帶了三匹驢子悄悄地離開，
在神奇的地點叫道：「芝麻開門！」那塊巨石便滾動開啓，兩匹驢子首先走入洞去，
第三匹驢子拒絕就範，卡深拉啊，拉啊，鞭打完又叫喊，直至那可憐的動物投降爲止，
但那驢子很憤怒，用全力踢向石頭，那巨石便慢慢地嘎扎的關上了。
「來啊，你這隻愚蠢的動物，」卡深咆哮著說。

That night, when everyone was asleep, Cassim slipped out of the village with three
donkeys. At the magic spot he called, "Open Sesame!" and the rock rolled open.
The first two donkeys went in, but the third refused to budge. Cassim tugged and tugged,
whipped and screamed until the poor beast gave in. But the donkey was so angry that it
gave an almighty kick against the rock and slowly the rock crunched shut.
"Come on, you stupid animal," growled Cassim.

在洞中，驚訝的卡深高興得透不過氣來，他快速地填滿一袋又一袋，
將它們高高的叠在可憐的驢子身上。當卡深不能再拿時，他便決定回家去。
他大聲叫道：「腰果開門！」沒有任何動靜。
「杏仁開門！」他叫道，又是沒有動靜。
「開心果開門！」依然沒有動靜。
卡深逐漸變得窘迫絕望，他叫喊和咒罵，他嘗試所有不同的方法，
但他就是記不起「芝麻」！
卡深和他那三匹驢子就被困在那裏。

Inside, an amazed Cassim gasped with pleasure. He quickly filled bag after bag, and piled them
high on the poor donkeys. When Cassim couldn't grab any more, he decided to go home.
He called out aloud, "Open Cashewie!" Nothing happened.
"Open Almony!" he called. Again, nothing.
"Open Pistachi!" Still nothing.
Cassim became desperate. He screamed and cursed as he tried every way possible,
but he just could not remember "Sesame"!
Cassim and his three donkeys were trapped.

第二天早上，阿里巴巴那憂慮異常的嫂子到來敲他的門。
「卡深還未回家，」她哭道，「他在那裏？啊，他究竟在那裏？」
阿里巴巴感到震驚，他到處尋找他的兄弟，直至他筋疲力盡爲止。
卡深會在那裏呢？
跟著他便想起了，他走去那塊大石處。卡深的身軀躺在山洞外，
沒有一點氣息，那群盜賊已先發現了他。
「一定要快快先把卡深下葬，」阿里巴巴一面想，
一面將他兄弟的沉重身軀擡回家。

Next morning a very upset sister-in-law came knocking on Ali Baba's door.
"Cassim has not come home," she sobbed. "Where is he? Oh, where is he?"
Ali Baba was shocked. He searched everywhere for his brother until he
was completely exhausted. Where could Cassim be?
Then he remembered.
He went to the place where the rock was. Cassim's lifeless body lay
outside the cave. The thieves had found him first.
"Cassim must be buried quickly," thought Ali Baba, carrying his brother's
heavy body home.

當那些大盜回來時，他們找不到屍體，可能是野獸把卡深拖走了，
但這是什麼腳印呢？
「有人知道我們的秘密，」卡伊大叫，又憤怒，又狂野。
「他也一定要死。」
那些盜賊跟著腳印一直來到送殯行列，那行列已向著阿里巴巴的家走去。
「一定是那裏了，」卡伊想著，靜靜地在前門畫上一個白色的圓圈。
「今晚等所有人都睡著了時，我便殺死他。」
但卡伊卻不知道有人看到他。

When the thieves returned they could not find the body. Perhaps wild
animals had carried Cassim away. But what were these footprints?
"Someone else knows of our secret," screamed Ka-eed, wild with anger.
"He too must be killed!"
The thieves followed the footprints straight to the funeral procession
which was already heading towards Ali Baba's house.
"This must be it," thought Ka-eed, silently marking a white circle on the
front door. "I'll kill him tonight, when everyone is asleep."
But Ka-eed was not to know that someone had seen him.

小婢摩姬安娜看到他，她覺得這個陌生人很邪惡。
「那圓圈究竟表示什麼呢？」她覺得很奇怪，並靜候著卡伊離開。
跟著摩姬安娜做了一件很聰明的事，她拿了粉筆，
在全村的所有門都畫上同樣的白圓圈。

The servant girl, Morgianna, was watching him. She felt this strange
man was evil. "Whatever could this circle mean?" she wondered and
waited for Ka-eed to leave. Then Morgianna did something really clever.
Fetching some chalk she marked every door in the village with the same
white circle.

That night the thieves silently entered the village when everyone was fast asleep.
"Here is the house," whispered one.
"No, here it is," said another.
"What are you saying? It is here," cried a third thief.
Ka-eed was confused. Something had gone terribly wrong, and he ordered his thieves to retreat.

那天晚上，當所有人都熟睡時，那些盜賊便靜悄悄的走入村去。

「就是這間屋，」其中一個低聲說。

「不，是這一間，」另一個說道。

「你說什麼？這間才是，」第三個大盜叫道。

卡伊覺得很混亂，情況變得十分不妥，於是他命令他的大盜退出村去。

第二天一早，卡伊返回村去，
他那修長的影子籠罩著阿里巴巴的屋子，
卡伊知道這便是他昨晚找不到的圓圈。
他想出一個計劃，
他會送四十個漂亮的瓷瓶給阿里巴巴，
但每個瓷瓶裏面都會有一個大盜，拿著劍，等候著。
那天稍後時間，摩姬安娜看到駱駝篷車和馬車駛向阿
里巴巴的屋前，她覺得很奇怪。

Early next morning Ka-eed came back.
His long shadow fell on Ali Baba's house and Ka-eed knew that this
was the circle he could not find the night before. He thought of a plan.
He would present Ali Baba with forty beautifully painted vases.
But inside each vase would be one thief, with his sword ready, waiting.
Later that day, Morgianna was surprised to see a caravan of camels,
horses and carriages draw up in front of Ali Baba's house.

一個穿著紫袍和頭裹輝煌的頭巾的男人來找她的主人。
「阿里巴巴，」那人說道，「你很聰明，找到你的兄弟，救了他，讓他免受野獸吞噬，這實在是勇敢的行爲，你應該得到獎賞，我們的酋長是庫古斯坦的貴族，他賞賜給你四十桶他最珍貴的珠寶。」
你到現在可能已知道阿里巴巴並不怎麼聰明，他笑著收下他的禮物。
「看呀，摩姬安娜，看我得到什麼，」他說。
但摩姬安娜則不以爲然，她感覺到可怕的事情即將發生。

A man in purple robes and magnificent turban called on her master.
"Ali Baba," the man said. "You are gifted. Finding and saving your brother from the fangs of wild animals is indeed a courageous act. You must be rewarded.
My sheikh, the noble of Kurgoostan, presents you with forty barrels of his most exquisite jewels."
You probably know by now that Ali Baba was not very clever and he accepted the gift with a wide grin.
"Look, Morgianna, look what I have been given," he said.
But Morgianna was not sure. She felt something terrible was going to happen.

「快，」當卡伊離去後，她大叫道，「給我煮三擔油，
直至油鑊冒出煙。快！否則便太遲了，我等一下才解釋。」
阿里巴巴很快便將嘶嘶地在煤炭上劈啪燃燒的原油拿來，
摩姬安娜將那邪惡的液體倒入提桶內，然後倒進第一個大桶去，
再將桶蓋緊緊地關上，那桶劇烈地搖動，差不多便要倒塌下來，
跟著它便不動了，摩姬安娜靜靜地打開桶蓋，阿里巴巴
便看到一個死了的盜賊！
當明白了詭計後，阿里巴巴便幫摩姬安娜
用同一種方法殺死所有的強盜。

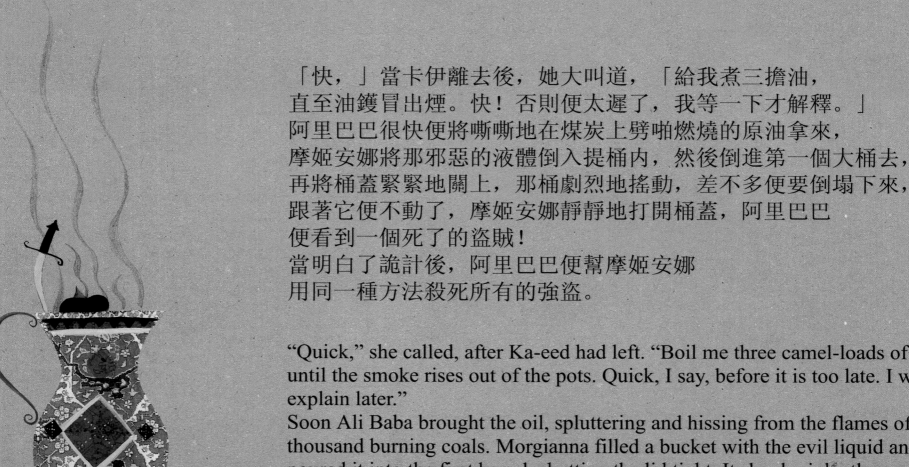

"Quick," she called, after Ka-eed had left. "Boil me three camel-loads of oil until the smoke rises out of the pots. Quick, I say, before it is too late. I will explain later."

Soon Ali Baba brought the oil, spluttering and hissing from the flames of a thousand burning coals. Morgianna filled a bucket with the evil liquid and poured it into the first barrel, shutting the lid tight. It shook violently, nearly toppling over. Then it became still. Morgianna quietly opened the lid and Ali Baba saw one very dead robber!

Convinced of the plot, Ali Baba helped Morgianna kill all the robbers in the same way.

那天晚上，卡伊到來與阿里巴巴飲宴，
他們大吃烹調特異的肉類和糕點麵包，飲豐盛的果子釀成的蜜酒。
但高潮卻是摩姬安娜的舞蹈表演！可憐的卡伊根本沒有翻身的機會，
美食飽餐後，他一面打嗝，一面望著摩姬安娜轉跳得越來越近。
突然，他感覺到一把鑲滿鑽石的匕首插進他的心。

That evening Ka-eed arrived to feast with Ali Baba.
They gorged on meats and breads cooked in wonderful ways.
They drank the rich nectar of sumptuous fruits.
But the highlight was Morgianna's dance! Poor Ka-eed did not
have a chance. Belching with the rich food, his eyes rolled
round and round watching Morgianna spin closer and closer.
Then all of a sudden, he felt a diamond studded dagger plunge
into the depths of his heart.

第二天，阿里巴巴返回那塊大石的地方，他把裏面秘藏的錢幣和珠寶都拿出來，
跟著便叫最後的一次：「芝麻關門！」
他將所有的珠寶分給群眾，他們推舉他為他們的領袖，
而阿里巴巴也封摩姬安娜為他的總參謀。

The next day Ali Baba returned to the place where the rock was. He emptied the cave
of its secret coins and jewels and he called out, "Close Sesame!" for the last time.
He gave all the jewels to the people, who made Ali Baba their leader.
And Ali Baba made Morgianna his chief adviser.